"Perhaps it was a flower
that made a painter out of me."
Claude Monet

© for the original French edition: L'Élan vert,
Paris, 2012
© for the English edition: Prestel Verlag,
Munich · London · New York, 2013

Library of Congress Control Number is available;
British Library Cataloguing-in-Publication Data:
a catalogue record for this book is available from
the British Library; Deutsche Nationalbibliothek
holds a record of this publication in the Deutsche
Nationalbibliografie; detailed bibliographical
data can be found under:
http://dnb.ddb.de.

Prestel Verlag, Munich
A member of Verlagsgruppe
Random House GmbH
www.prestel.com

English translation: Agathe Joly

Editing: Cynthia Hall
Typesetting: textum GmbH, Munich
Production: Astrid Wedemeyer
Printing and binding: TBB, a. s.

Verlagsgruppe Random House FSC-DEU-0100
The FSC-certified paper *Hello Fat Matt*
was supplied by Deutsche Papier.

Printed in Slovakia

ISBN 978-3-7913-7139-9

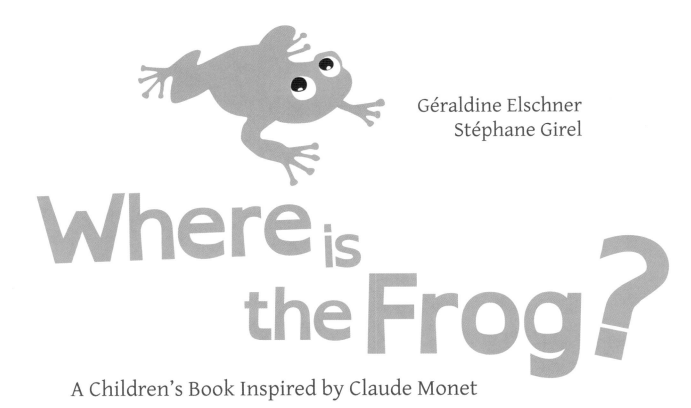

Géraldine Elschner
Stéphane Girel

Where is the Frog?

A Children's Book Inspired by Claude Monet

Prestel
Munich · London · New York

— Look out: a frog hunter!

Without a moment's hesitation, Antoinette hops between
the irises and vanishes deep beneath the water.
— **Calm down, gargoyle,** groans a toad.

There's no need to worry!
The man only sketches flowers.
He doesn't eat frogs' legs.

Flowers?
Did someone say Flowers?
Antoinette slips from her hiding place and admires her reflection in the water.

— In that case, I'm the perfect catch, come and take a look! Seriously, I'm at least as pretty as a **water lily** ... just a little mint leaf in the water. From the corner of her eye, she watches the old man standing among the poppies.

Mister Claude ...

A white beard and a bunch of brushes, an easel and a hat.
The great flower hunter seems to be looking for something.

The painter walks slowly back and forth in the garden.

A **daisy** *here,*
a **dahlia** *there* ...

He lightly touches the petals, glances up at the sky,
and adjusts the flowers.

He stops at the foot of the little bridge
and sets up his stool and easel.

It's now or never!
Just as Mister Claude pulls out his painting tubes and
sets up his palette, **hop!** Antoinette leaps onto a water lily.
The coquette powders the tip of her nose and then she's ready.

Careful,
don't **move** a muscle! But ...

... first her right leg starts to tickle
and then her left. How can she pose
without wriggling when it feels
like she has springs beneath her feet **?**

Ouch! Antoinette is about to give up when ... **phew**
The church bell rings and the painter leaves for lunch.
Free at last! The poor little frog hobbles back to the bridge
to admire her portrait in the finished sketch.

But ...

...where's the frog?

— **By Jove,** what a fool I am **!**
Green on green:
of course, you can't see a thing!

The following day, the sun is high in the sky
by the time Mister Claude comes down to the garden.
He brings a basket to his studio boat.
Antoinette leaps onto a nearby dinghy, **Hop, hop !**

But ... ...where's
the **frog?**

— **Good gracious,**
these twigs need trimming!

A few days later, in the shade of an old willow tree,
the white-bearded man gazes at the water lilies.
Antoinette, perched on a branch, sways and swings
in the wind. **But ...**

— **Are** those **your little frog legs** I see **?**

taunts a heron with an appetite.

If so, I could eat them in one gulp!

After a fright like that, **Antoinette** is exhausted.
Spotting a nest at the foot of the willow tree,
she climbs in and falls right asleep.

—— Hey! There's something in my hat! exclaims the surprised painter.
How funny, I almost mistook it for a green water lily.
And he picks up his brush.
When Antoinette wakes up she can't believe her eyes.

There, on the canvas, right in front ... there she is at last! **She's** become the muse, the nymph, the queen of this flowery garden.

How **beautiful** she **looks!**

— Come close so that I can kiss you,
says Antoinette to the portrait facing her.
She quickly jumps towards the canvas and ...

everything tumbles into the water:
the easel, the brushes, the frog, and her picture.
Antoinette was never seen again.

And Mister Claude never really got over it.
The masterpiece has **remained** missing ever since ...

Claude Monet
(1840-1926)

page 7

Yellow Irises
c. 1914–17, oil on canvas
200 x 150 cm
Fondation Beyeler, Bâle, Switzerland
© Artothek / Hans Hinz

page 9

An Alley in Monet's Garden, Giverny
c. 1901–02, oil on canvas
89 x 92 cm
Österreichische Galerie Belvedere,
Vienna, Austria
© Artothek / Photobusiness

page 10

The Water Lily Pond
1899, oil on canvas
89.5 x 91.5 cm
Private collection, Tokyo, Japan
© Artothek / Peter Willi

page 13

Water Lily, Night Effects
1897, oil on canvas
73 x 100 cm
Musée Marmottan, Paris
© Bridgeman-Giraudon

page 14

The Water Lily Pond
1904, oil on canvas
90 x 92 cm
Musée des Beaux-Arts, Caen
© Artothek / Peter Willi

page 17

The Boat
1887, oil on canvas
146 x 133 cm
Musée Marmottan, Paris
© Artothek / Peter Willi

page 18

Blue Water Lilies
1916–19, oil on canvas
200 x 200 cm
Musée d'Orsay, Paris
© Artothek / Christie's Images Ltd.

page 21

Water Lilies
c. 1905, oil on canvas
89 x 101 cm
Private collection
© Artothek / Christie's Images Ltd.

Who was "Mister Claude"?

Born in Paris in 1840, Claude Monet became famous when he moved to Giverny in 1883. He remained there until his death in 1926 and would become one of the great masters of Impressionism. Like Renoir, Manet, Pissaro, and others, he tried to capture a specific moment and the effect of light rather than an actual subject. In 1874, his painting *Impression: Sun Rise* gave the movement Impressionism its name.

How did he paint nature?

In 1850, the manufacturing of tubes of oil paint dramatically changed the life of painters. Convenient and lightweight, just like the new easels that were being built, the tubes could be closed again after use, allowing artists to venture out of the studio and study their subjects "en plein air," or out in the open. Nature became a vast studio filled with bright and shimmering colors. Like his friend Eugène Boudin, Monet now began to set up his easels wherever he fancied: in the country, on the cliffs of Normandy, by the waterside ...

Water and sky...

Whether it was foggy or sunny, the reflections of light on the water were a great subject for these painters who did not seek to capture the exact thing they saw, but rather the distinct impression it created with each passing moment. Monet watched the shadow of leaves in the calm waters of his pond at Giverny, the white winter light on the frozen Seine river, the brightness of the summer sun when it bathed his studio-boat in Argenteuil, and the sky and the way it changed above the waves—as in *La Manneporte, Reflections on the Water* (1885-86) and *The Beach of Sainte-Adresse* (1867).

Giverny, the perfect studio!

Yes! Here nature was no longer wild. It was created entirely by Monet, who would compose the landscapes of his paintings himself. In his garden, he gave life to what he wanted to paint: flowers, chosen with the utmost care, were nurtured by several gardeners, and water was diverted from a nearby stream to feed the pond, which he dug close to the house. A gardener and a painter, he loved this place with all his heart. "The doors open onto paradise," said one of his friends. Monet planted the scenery; there he would also plant his easel almost every day for the rest of his life.

A true palette of flowers

... and of colors. Irises, nasturtiums, roses, dahlias, peonies ... the varieties of flowers were infinite. Bamboo and Japanese bridges completed the ensemble. Monet's palette varied according to the time of day and the season. An early riser, he worked in his garden for hours, catching every nuance of light through the days and across the water. The palette he used can be found in the Musée Marmottan and in many ways it resembles his pond.

Were water lilies Monet's favorite subject matter?

One of his favorites, in any case. Monet made more than 300 paintings in this water garden, where he attempted to decompose light and represent water lilies, sometimes surrounded by greenery (*Water Lily Pond*), sometimes beneath a bridge (*Japanese Bridge*), and sometimes even spreading across the entire canvas (*Waterscapes*). He liked to paint the same motif at different times and in different light, in order to capture the fleeting effects: he painted a series of haystacks, for example, and depicted the Cathedral of Rouen at dawn, noon, sunset, and nighttime ... a total of eighteen times.

Why such a gigantic painting of water lilies?

From 1914 to 1918, in the midst of World War I, Monet painted day and night despite his old age and the cataracts that made him go almost blind. He wanted to create a haven of peace. The gigantic and circular panels in the Orangerie, a museum located in the Tuileries Garden in Paris, invite us into a peaceful landscape, into Monet's dream of harmony, which he presented to his country as "a monument to Man's interior peace." A symbol of life, the water lilies become immortal. "I find myself in the center of an enchanted pond," said Monet as he painted them. The same impression can be felt today in contemplating them.